The Rainbow Bubble Collapse

Fantasy Short Story

for me

The Rainbow Bubble Collapse

Fantasy Short Story

Topaz Hauyn

Visit us online:
www.topazhauyn.com

Copyright ©2022 by Topaz Hauyn
c/o Lösche, Lehenbühlstr. 55, 71272 Renningen, Germany
All rights reserved.

ISBN: 9798408891191
Font: Alegreya
Coverdesign: Topaz Hauyn
Art: ddraw/depositphotos.com

This book is licensed for your personal enjoyment only.
This is a work of fiction. All characters and events portrayed in this book are fictional, and any
resemblance to real people or incidents is purely coincidental.
This book, or parts thereof, may not be reproduced in any form without permission.

The seven colors of the rainbow wrapped in circles around the many bubbles floating through the air. The bright green was her favorite, like spring was her favorite season. The season of new beginnings and hope.

Tabia watched two soap bubbles nearing each other until their colors merged in a whirlwind of waltz. Like the colors of the dresses worn in ballroom dance competitions.

Her last competition dress had been dark purple, chosen by her father to underline her families power.

Purple was the color of their house. Nobody in the city dared to were purple, except for them. Although, as her white-haired, teacher Mr. Briga reminded her regularly, Hemrun was a democratic city.

Tabia liked the floor-length, sparkling dresses with their many layers of fine fabric. Often silk. But the dark purple one she despised. She got out of step on purpose, ruining the performance of their choreography.

She would never do something similar again.

Describing her father as being upset and angry was an understatement even her mother declared as such.

Therefore, she wasn't allowed outside. Except with private guards and only to attend her classes.

Tabia thought of her dance partner. Horror ran through her body asking herself what might have happened to him.

Her dance partner had vanished after the competition and never showed up again. Instead, a new man appeared at her dance training: Reimar Angeer.

Reimar was taller than even her father and towered her by two heads. He had muscles were normal dancers had none. And his piercing blue eyes didn't fit his black hair.

Tabia closed her eyes and thought of his firm hands, leading her over the dance floor in plain signals with his whole body. The minimal, perfectly measured pressure of his hand against hers, or against her back, was exceptional.

None, not even her dance teachers, Mr. Theo Dear and Mrs. Lara, rose perfume is my second name, Dear, ever provided her such a perfect lead.

Blowing soap bubbles was Tabia's second favorite action to fill her leisure time. They were light and free and always changing, while she was none of this.

Clumsy beyond the dance floor with her surplus wight, imprisoned by her father, constantly lectured on her eating habits and always dressed up to a sparkling beauty. To uphold the family pride, her mother said.

As if the family pride was the only thing that mattered.

Being a member of the Maninga family in the city, she wasn't allowed to hang out with whomever she wanted to. Instead, she met the people her father had-selected to support his power.

The merged soap bubble, now became one.

The colors settled except for the green. It disturbed the rainbow swirling around the bubble into two swirls going clockwise and anticlockwise.

Could she ever do the same? Like her older sister, whose name had been removed from the family tree and the public memory.

Even Tabia herself didn't know her name. The fact that she knew about this older sister was a declaration of war enough for her father. Therefore, she never mentioned anything about her.

Tabia felt the plastic, she held to blow new bubbles, hard in her hand. She wanted to add some more, but there was no more bubble liquid in the circular bottle.

She leaned back against the cushioned backrest of the soft, purple sofa in her living room.

Looking upside was more comfortable now, than sitting upright with her head craned upwards, to watch the bubbles collapse one after the other.

Finally, only the huge, merged bubble floated through the air towards the white ceiling with the grape stucco ornaments.

Tabia heard a low blob, when the bubble met the tip of a grape leave. It burst, sending sparkling pieces of the rainbow around the room, like sparkling fireworks.

The grape winked at her, revealing a bright blue eye looking down at her, winking.

Tabia blinked.

The grape stucco ornament didn't move. It was white and unchanged as before.

Or again?

She started to daydream about her new dance partner again. How awful, for she knew perfectly well, that he used her as a tool to gain more influence in the city.

Being seen with one of the Maninga family gave one a lot of influence with the right people. Or so he told her.

She put the soap bubble stick and bottle on the round glass table next to the sofa, picked up her university school book about programming in Pyt and flipped it open at the torn off piece of paper bookmark.

She couldn't remember the times, when her father had to win elections to stay in place. Or times when technology advanced. She only knew about it from tales and schoolbooks. Those times were only about three decades ago.

Time to study. She wanted to support herself soon, leave the family estate and move to another city. Maybe she could find her sister one day.

After two pages, a knock at the door interrupted Tabia's concentration.

"Yes, please?", said Tabia.

She saw the door handle moved down.

The door, decorated with the same grape leaves as the ceiling stucco, swung open noiseless.

In the black door frame, fitting his black hair, so it seemed he stepped out of the frame itself, stood Reimar, wearing his black dance suit. The red shirt with the purple tie, a gift from her father Tafil.

"You're late to our training", said Reimar with a low voice.

His blue eyes met hers and hold them without blinking.

She felt his presence floating from the door through the room and sat up straight.

Tabia knew she was dressed perfectly in her favorite, green, floor-length, sleeveless dress. Her brown hair was braided and decorated with little diamond flowers.

The sunlight falling into her room from the window on her left surely let the diamonds sparkle.

"There is no training today", said Tabia.

Having Reimar walking through her living room was a new, unsettling experience. She felt like he tried to take over her place. Something about his step was off. Not as well-balanced as usually.

"Now there is", said Reimar.

His smile lit up his face, made it even more beautiful than before.

She tried to focus back on her book, yet only saw meaningless, black signs on the page.

Tabia glanced through the open door on the side to her little kitchen. Usually she ate with her family, but sometimes, especially late at night, she cooked a snack for herself.

Always hungry at night. The reason she wore surplus clothing.

She thought about her sharp knifes.

What if she used one to cut the unwelcome intruder out of her home?

Tabia imagined how Reimar would look at her guiding him outside with her kitchen knife. She felt a smile bloom on her face.

Then, she decided this wasn't the time to fight her new dance partner. Her father wouldn't be pleased to find his dead body in her living room.

"Well then. I will meet you there in a few minutes", said Tabia with her best you-are-dismissed-voice.

A deep laughter filled the room.

"Looking forward to you", said Reimar.

He winked at her.

Reimar was gone.

Not in the walking-out-of-the-door-style-gone, but in the poof-vanished-style-gone.

Tabia stared at the empty spot half-way between the stucco embroidered door and her seating place.

The door still stood open, giving her a free sight on the purple carpet running down the hall, together with the lilac flowers covering the walls between the painting hanging on both sides.

The smell of soap and fresh cleaned carpets breezed into her room. Her green carpet needed cleaning too. It started to smell a little dusty.

Tabia got up, closed the door and opened the windows for fresh air.

She stared at the birch trees in front of her. White, slender and beautiful with their long slender branches and green leaves. They danced with the wind, as she danced with the orchestra's tunes in the ballroom. Her happy moments.

The wind brushed over her face, helped her return to her thoughts.

Did she know anybody who could use magic to send himself to a distant place?

Nobody, was the honest answer.

She had seen it happen. Who would be able to conjure such magic, or illusion?

Witches? No, they were only female, and besides, part of the fairy tales. Nothing real.

Fairies? Fairy tales, too.

Did she underestimate his speed?

Tabia thought about Reimar who moved through the ballroom a few weeks back.

One moment he had been on the other end of the hall amidst a group of powerful, gray-haired men, chatting, making connections to politicians. Then, shortly before her father stepped through one of the many doors, Reimar had been at her side.

Her father's presence always announced him an instant before he actually stepped through a door into a room. Like a wave of power clearing his way for him.

The music had been a constant background sound, often drowned by the chatter, the noise of many steps and the rustling of clothes. Although she watched Reimar the whole time, angry for being left alone. When she was ready to march through the room and publicly blame him for ignoring his duties, he had appeared at her side. Together with two glasses of orange juice, offering her one.

Her father had stepped through the door and looked at her.

He always did. Not seeking out her mother, but her. Like making sure she hadn't done something stupid in his absence.

So, she took the cool glass, Reimar offered her. The orange juice had smelled fresh and fruity. Its taste had been sweet and a bit sour on her tongue. A welcome change from the dry, hot air in the ballroom.

She remembered her raised hackles from Reimar's sudden appearance. She had successfully fought her urge to gulp the juice down. She had held her glass with two fingers, had managed to sip it mannerly. And like today, any thoughts about Reimar's behavior had slipped away.

Her fathers gaze had lingered.

She still felt the sight of her father tingling on her face, together with his final approving nod. Her father hadn't looked at her again that evening. Thankfully, convinced she behaved herself. Back then she hadn't thought about how Reimar managed to pass this fast through a ballroom full of people.

Even sprinting through the empty ballroom would have taken her longer.

Not to think of the people he had to weave through.

The fresh air greeted Tabia as she stepped through the open door on the polished dance floor. It filled the whole room. Her dance shoes made a low sound on the floor with each step.

The sun, falling through the open windows, drew circles and rectangles on the floor. The artsy mobile hanging from the ceiling spread the light into all directions like the firework of light her bubbles provided earlier in her living room.

The scent of polished wood filled the room, reminding her of the many happy hours she spent dancing on them.

Waltz music was played through the loudspeakers as background sound.

She felt herself huge and skilled in this environment.

The dance floor was Tabia's home.

The place she sparkled willingly. The place she escaped the constant criticism of her father. Her surplus weight didn't matter here. Not with the layers of sparkling silk and the long, swooshing dresses, designed to show the elegance and beauty inherent in each living being. Together with the dim light in the evenings, the shadows gracefully made her seem a more slender danseuse on the stage. A person sparkling with skill, joy, and family support.

Another world.

An illusion.

Created for the outsiders, to support her father's success.

For her father, being the major of a huge city like Hemrun, counting half a million inhabitants was a huge success. A majority voted for Tafil Maninga for decades now.

Staying the major was his only goal, although he managed skillfully to tell every citizen his goal was to make their living easier.

And by easier, Tafil the major, usually meant, less competition in the city hall. Smaller opposition, larger ruling party.

Tabia always wondered, how the people of Hemrun couldn't see through the spectacle her father played in front of them.

She had no choice but to follow his rules. With nobody seeing her fathers schemes, there was nobody she could trust.

The citizens might have friends helping them if a demonstration failed. She had nobody. Not even her missing sister.

Had her sister found friends helping her? Or was she dead?

Angry at her thoughts, they never led to a result telling her how to move on, she decided to ignore them for now.

This was her room of joy, not of worries.

Tabia smiled at Reimar in her best the-show-must-go-on smile.

He stood at the other side, next to the wall between two windows. The vine leave stucco was painted purple and green in the dance hall.

He connected his smartphone to the music device. His back in black suite was towards Tabia.

She smiled nonetheless.

Her image to the others was important, it was the currency she had. The currency her father used.

A lot.

"Which dance first?", asked Tabia.

Reimar changed the slow waltz to a Viennese waltz. Turned and met Tabia at the center of the room.

She laid her hand in his warm, soft hand. She put her other hand on the silk fabric of his suit jacket. It felt cooler than his hand.

The intro of the song passed.

Tabia listened to the piano and violins.

Then, Reimar led her into natural turns around the dance floor.

"Glad you could make it", whispered Reimar.

"I am sorry I forgot our appointment", said Tabia.

She floated through the room following his lead into a spot turn and multiple reverse turns before returning to the natural turns.

She smelled Reimar sweating. Which was something new. He never overexerted himself during their dance lessons. And this was the first dance to warm up.

"Where are our teachers today?", asked Tabia.

Tabia knew Reimar's technique was perfect. He was exact on the beat with the music. His lead was perfect, too. Yet, something was missing.

Her former dance partner had managed to give the dance meaning and emotion. Something Tabia rarely experienced in her starchy world filled with political considerations at each step.

Reimar had never shown the slightest hint of feelings.

Not for the music, for he followed a given choreography, no matter which music he chose for a dance. Not for the woman he led through the room.

He looked past her head, as she did in her pose, slightly leaned backwards, head turned to the left, neck stretched elegant.

He sweated more. She could see the little beads of sweat on his forehead.

"Our teachers have no time today", said Reimar. "But we can do without them, can't we?"

Tabia turned her head and stared into Reimar's eyes. Their deep blue was shadowy today. Something bothered her perfect, cool dance partner.

"What's the matter with you today?", asked Tabia.

He led her into a whisk.

"My brother returned today", said Reimar. "Stay away from him. He's dangerous."

Tabia forced herself to control her face. She managed to only slightly raise her eyebrow and not shout her surprise in his face.

"You never told me about your family. Why would your brother be dangerous?", asked Tabia.

She couldn't imagine a reason, this brother of Reimar could become a threat to her. Neither in the sunny daylight she danced in, nor in the dimmer evening events and dances held at this house by her father.

"He's a rebel. He wants to stage a coup against your father", whispered Reimar. "Never mix me with him. Please."

Tabia's eyes widened a bit. Feeling from Reimar? That was news to her. He led her into spot turns and some quick changes of directions. She observed him searching the room for listeners.

Was he afraid of his brother, or . . .

"You're afraid of being held accountable for him", asked Tabia.

Reimar didn't answer, but Tabia was quite sure.

"How will he approach me?", asked Tabia.

"I don't know", said Reimar. "He's different from me."

Tabia put one foot after the other, following the dance. She continued doing so through their whole training.

She thought about the eye in the stucco leaves at her living room. Had that been Reimar's brother?

"Your brother is supernatural", said Tabia at the end of their training, with the music still on. "He can see through walls."

It wasn't meant as a question.

Reimar answered anyway: "He's a magician. He can do more than merely see through walls."

She watched him rake his fingers through his hair. The neatly combed hairstyle turned into a messy one.

She didn't like Reimar, especially not after getting him as a lifeless replacement for her former dance partner of her fathers choosing.

Therefore, she ignored his obvious agony and kept asking:

"What else can he do?", asked Tabia.

"Run along with my dear brother. Unseen as his shadow", said a voice behind her.

Tabia got out of step, turned and searched for the voice. There was nobody, beside Reimar's shadow thrown on the floor by the sunlight.

Tabia felt Reimar hands on her waist, pulling her backwards and pushing her aside, off his shadow.

The music continued playing in the background as if nothing had happened.

But something had happened.

Tabia suddenly was well aware, that she hadn't day-dreamed earlier in her living room. There had been a blue eye in the stucco leaves near the ceiling.

Probably it had been this shadow brother.

She had a hunch she should run. Try to escape. Feel frightened.

No, she decided. Not today. There were enough secrets already. She wanted to investigate this one.

Safety, such a superficial word. Everyone used it around her. Used it to imprison her in this mansion, in her rooms.

"Leave, it's not safe for you. I try to put a stop to him", said Reimar.

He didn't look as confident as his words sounded.

Tabia saw Reimar's hands shaking.

She smiled her most innocent smile and ignored his order.

"Why don't you introduce me?", asked Tabia with her sweetest voice. "One can fight a known danger better than a mystery."

She watched the Reimar's shadow on the floor.

It moved, grew, slid sideways and formed a figure on the floor, right next to the shadow of Reimar.

"No. Run!", ordered Reimar.

The shadow stretched out its hand and tipped at Tabia's shadow's shoulder.

She felt the tap on her shadows shoulder as if there was a man next to her, tapping with an ice cube on her shoulder.

She shrugged it off.

No way! She would not allow this magician to scare her with such a simple trick!

"Behave yourself! What do you want?", said Tabia.

The shadow laughed. It sounded like a storm rustling through treetops.

"I love your new dance partner, dear brother. She has more fire than your last one. Did you tell her about her sister, Katherine already?", asked the shadow.

He spoke with the light voice, that could easily blend in with the low rustling of wind through the branches of the birches outside Tabia's living room window.

"Don't you dare", said Reimar, clearly trying to stop his brother.

Tabia put her hand on his upper arm to hold him back.

"What do you know about Katherine?", asked Tabia.

"Nothing", said Reimar.

He pulled his arm from her grip.

"Well. It seems different, given your brothers words", said Tabia.

She crossed her arms in front of her chest. The silk on her back stretched. It was sewn to fit her standing casually or dancing, her arms stretched out. There wasn't enough material to allow crossing for long.

She heard a crack in the fabric at her back. A bad sound.

She carefully, slowly unfolded her arms.

Looking beautiful wasn't worth it, if you couldn't express your annoyance properly, decided Tabia.

She settled with tapping her toes in her dance shoes on the floor, making an impatient sound.

Not as good as her former position, but surely not damaging her dress.

"Katherine is with the rebels", said the shadow. "She sent me to warn you. And only you. Maybe we can speak at another place. Alone."

Tabia nodded. Her sister sent word to her. Her heart beat hard against her chest. Maybe there was a chance she could finally escape her father. She felt hope rise. Hope she couldn't allow blooming too much or else the disappointment would be too much to keep going.

"Don't. He'll kidnap you. They need a victim to blackmail your father", said Reimar.

He stepped between Tabia and the shadow.

"Why would they do so if my father is doing as fine as everyone thinks?", asked Tabia.

She knew her father didn't and would do a lot to outmaneuver blackmail. The question was, was she valuable enough to him? Katherine hadn't been and, therefore, vanished. There was barely any trace left from her existence.

"They are mean. They can't accept that they didn't score the well paying jobs. They begrudge everyone who has success", said Reimar, talking faster and faster with each word. "See, they couldn't leave me alone; having success becoming a well paid dancer; no they threatened me; took away my life, my career, and now they took you and your life."

Tabia saw Reimar's shoulders shake from the fast talking.

Was he crying? His voice sounded a bit like it.

"Now your going melodramatic, dear brother. It doesn't suit you", said the shadow. "Besides. You're wrong. This gig isn't well paying. Actually it pays nothing, because your expenses are higher than your salary."

That sparked a memory of a conversation, Tabia overheard some weeks back.

She had been early for her training and heard her father talk to Reimar. She didn't search his presence for it meant more criticism about her weight. Therefore, she stayed outside the door, eavesdropping a bit.

They had talked about payments. Reimar had asked for a pay rise to cover the expensive suits he needed.

She remembered how her father had refused it by simply saying, a good dancer is worth nothing if he couldn't keep up with his audience.

The next evening at the dance floor, Reimar's suit had been even more expensive than before.

Tabia hadn't wondered that much back then. But now things got clearer. She guessed, Reimar hadn't gotten the pay rise, although he wore more expensive suits.

"So, what do you expect by this job aside from debts?", asked Tabia.

"Visibility", said Reimar in a sad voice.

Although, Reimar was two heads taller than Tabia, he looked smaller than her now. With his shoulders hanging like the ones of a beaten man, who just realized his answer had been the wrong one.

"Did it work?", asked Tabia.

She knew so little about the outside world.

Money never had been a problem. If she really ripped her dress by crossing her arms, her father would be angry about her being careless. But sure as dawn he would order a new dress and pay for it.

If only she could stand her fathers constant admonitions regarding her clumsiness and her surplus weight that followed each dress disaster.

"No", said the light shadowy voice. "He's so clamped in his work here, he can't make contacts in the ballroom to use his enlarged visibility."

Tabia felt bad for being angry at Reimar when he had talked to others in the ball-room. She always thought he was having fun, when he really tried to work on his career.

"Poor brother", said the shadow in a mock voice. "You should know better than that. Now, Tabia, where can we talk alone?"

"In my living room", said Tabia. "See you tomorrow at our official training, Reimar."

Reimar nodded silently. His eyes were dark and empty.

Tabia felt bad for leaving him behind beaten and discouraged. Yet, it was his decision to work for her father, wasn't it?

She curtsied her goodbye to Reimar and left the ballroom.

Sometime during their talk, the music came to a halt.

Tabia's steps echoed through the huge room until she stepped into the hall and the stuffy air coming from the old carpets there.

Tabia breathed in the fresh, warm air in her living room, after closing the stucco grape embroidered door behind her.

That was so much better than the stuffy air in the hall. She even liked her light room with the huge windows way more than the hall with the old paintings.

Her windows still stood open, and she heard the wind rustle through the leaves of the birches in front of it. Her schoolbook waited on the oval glass table next to her sofa. Tabia fetched a pair of glasses and a bottle of fresh, cold tab water from her kitchen. She moved the book aside and placed the water and the glasses there.

She evened the skirt of her dress and sat down.

She waited for Reimar's shadow brother.

How long would he need to follow her?

"Are you there?", asked Tabia.

She looked up to the stucco grapes at the white ceiling, where she had seen the blue eye, similar to Reimar's blue eyes, earlier today. But the stucco grapes were white as usual.

"Thank you for your invitation", said a foreign voice from the window. It was deeper than the airy shadow voice.

Tabia turned her head, feeling her dress stretching around her shoulders again.

So, he really was some kind of sorcerer. What else existed in her city she didn't know about?

Tabia thought about her last trip to the city to go shopping for her schoolbooks.

Her mother had accompanied her, making it a marketing campaign for their family, with the subtext: Look we're normal. We're working, learning and buying a book like everyone else.

She had seen lots of cameras taking pictures. The bookshops had been filled to the last inch with journalists, observing and recording each of her glances. Noting accurately which books she touched, flipped through and finally bought.

Needless to say she stayed away from the fiction bookshelves and picked the obligatory books for her university courses as fast as she could.

From the car she only saw the neat and clean fronts of the houses.

Only one spot wasn't clean. A corner where a child in ripped clothes had looked at her. Straight into her eyes, like it saw through all of her clothes, jewelry and make up.

This glance, however brief, haunted her ever since. Children should have proper clothes in her opinion.

When she drew her mothers attention to the child, she only waved and one of the security team surrounding their car had, maintaining a low profile, sent the child away.

Tabia had cursed herself. She probably could be thankful that was all her mother did, remembering how her former dance partner had vanished.

Which brought her thoughts back to her visitor. Reimar had warned her about his brother. Called him dangerous.

He leaned against one of the open window glasses. He did not look dangerous.

He was a man about two heads taller than her, probably a Reimar's twin, with the same piercing blue eyes. Only his black hair was longer than that of his brother, and it hung around in small curls freely.

The man wore a suit, similar to the one Reimar wore back in the ballroom today. Therefore, he was great at imitating other peoples clothes.

Tabia wanted to touch this man's face, trace the lines at the sides of his lips making it look gaunt.

Touching the curls that tempted her to comb and coiffure them. Many of the women she knew would envy him for this magnificent head of hair.

"My name is Tabia Manning", said Tabia.

She folded her hands neatly in her lap, waiting for him to follow the rules of courtesy.

It wasn't following the rules of courtesy to welcome a foreign man in her apartment, but, alas, one could make exceptions and follow the majority of the rules. Only her father never must learn about this.

"I am Patrizian Angeer", said the man. "Call me Pat, like all my friends. Please."

Was he a friend of hers?

Tabia decided, he was, if he was able to tell her something about her older sister. Something her father would definitely hate. Like he hated her modern kitchen with the stainless steel surfaces that didn't fit to the old style mansion. Or better, weren't to his taste.

"Why did your brother see you as a threat? Do you really plan to overthrow my fathers reign?", asked Tabia. "You are Reimar's twin, Pat. Right?"

Pat walked over and picked up one glass of water from the table.

He now stood in front of her.

Tabia had to crane her neck to see his face.

"Sit down", she ordered.

Craning her neck hurt, especially with her hairstyle: Heavy jewelry dragging the back of her head down to earth.

Pat snapped his fingers.

Tabia's jewelry got lighter instantly. She stared at him a moment in amazement.

"Thank you", said Tabia.

"Don't thank me", said Pat. "I'm taking what I like, and replacing your jewelry with light fake stones benefits me a lot."

Pat sat down next to her on the sofa.

His wight made her slip into his direction.

She caught herself and made an effort to stay at her place. She should be angry, knowing he stole from her without touching her, even admitting the crime.

However, she was happier with the light fake jewelry.

His scent was different from Reimar's. Pat smelled of dirt, sweat and fresh air.

Tabia knew this scent.

Wrinkling her nose, she thought, Pat had replaced his brother at least at one training session.

"Yes, my dear brother is my twin", said Reimar. "And I replaced him, when he got sick this last spring."

"You read my mind! Stop it!".

She leaned forward, feeling anger pulse through her body. Better she controlled her thoughts. A man disguising himself as a shadow, reading her thoughts was a threat. Indeed.

And she wasn't willing to let him steal her thoughts, too.

"I'm not. Your face gives your thoughts away", said Pat.

Tabia put on her public face with the huge smile. The one that made her cheeks ache at the end of each night after dinner and dancing. Tabia leaned back.

"What do you know about Katherine?", asked Tabia.

Sitting in her dress after dancing and sweating herself was uncomfortable. She'd rather wanted to go to the shower and dress more casually. Maybe in a few minutes.

"She's living with my mother. Hiding at another city from your father. She's fine and asked me to rescue you", said Pat

"Rescue me?", said Tabia. She sat up straight again. The silk of her dress rustled low. "I'm fine here."

"Don't you say. You're sure?", asked Pat.

Tabia's phone rung.

A a short message from her guards.

"Waiting for you in the courtyard with the car."

An order from her father. Probably another round or representative shopping, opening a kindergarten or some other stuff that kept the people respelled by his reportedly work to make their life better.

Additionally, she had to live through another afternoon of admonitions while sitting in the closed, black car with him.

The thought got her hackles up.

Tabia picked up her glass of water with both hands and took a sip.

"Why did my sister hide? What crime did she commit?", asked Tabia.

"She refused marrying the husband her father chose", said Pat. "This man will be your husband soon. The newspapers declared your engagement this morning."

Tabia stared at Pat. She heard him wrong, right?

She wasn't engaged. Had told her father she would never marry. Especially not to help his career as city major.

She felt her mouth hung open. Felt the fresh air cool her teeth.

She made an effort to close her mouth, only to find, she had dropped her glass. Her dress was wet from the knees down to the floor. Shards laid at her feet. She hadn't even heard the impact on the floor.

Another ring from her phone delivered a second message.

Her fingers shook, when she picked up the phone to read the message: "Pronto, your fiancée is waiting. Tafil."

Did her father just saved the word 'future' in his short message? He was never polite with her.

She threw the phone back on the glass table, where it hit forcefully, leaving a scratch.

One she liked a lot of seeing there.

Tabia glanced at Pat. He still sat next to her on the sofa.

"Prove me you didn't lie", said Pat.

She felt he was right. Somehow, she didn't want to believe her father did this to her: Flat out ignoring her decision.

Pat produced a newspaper from inside his black jacket. It was her fathers preferred newspaper: The Hamrum's News.

Bold letters on the first page, together with a picture from her and Kai Unsold greeting each other at one of the evening events, told her about her engagement.

The one she never agreed to.

The black of the ink blurred.

Tabia felt hot tears springing to her eyes.

She forced the tears back. There was no time for crying. Not with the option to escape her father once and for all, at hand.

Her father waited in the courtyard.

Pat declared to be here to rescue her, acting on a plea of her unknown sister Katherine.

"How can I get out of this prison?", asked Tabia.

She gestured around the room, meaning the whole mansion.

With the decision made, she felt lighter than she had for years.

Tabia's smartphone, on the oval glass table, rung.

Again.

Probably another short message.

She felt no desire to read Tafil's orders anymore. The man who chased her out of her home and stripped her off her family with his behavior, wasn't worth her time.

Dressed in her favorite green long sleeve and a pair of rough brown trousers, Pat gave her, Tabia returned from her bedroom.

She looked around her living room for one last time. She would miss the white stucco grapes and her university books to become a programmer.

Leaving now meant she would never graduate at the Hemrun state university, which was the guarantee to score a high paying employment.

She gulped. She had liked her teachers.

Pat stood at the open window. Waiting for her. The birch trees, she had planted as a child at his back.

She looked at them closely, branding them on her memory. She would come back and see them again.

One day.

On the day she liberated the city from Tafil.

Pat had given her a black, rough sack. It's cords now rubbed against her palms sensitive skin, as she walked over the soft carpet.

The sack was heavy from her casual clothes, the cash she had and her bottle of water.

No ID card or other cards though. Her father could track and find her through them.

Pat helped her put her arms through the two strings attached to the black sack to hang it on her back.

He took both of her hands in his big, warm ones

"I am glad you decided to leave", said Pat.

Tabia looked up in Pat's face.

With her hair braided it wasn't this painful like before to crane her neck.

"I feared to come back empty-handed, telling your sister bad news. Because this transportation spell only works if the second person agrees to being transported", said Pat.

Tabia nodded. "I agree. Bring me to my sister, please."

She heard her smartphone ringing again. This time it didn't stop.

In the distance she heard running through the corridors. An absolute no-go.

They came to fetch her.

"Leave now", said Tabia, her voice tight with urgency.

She grabbed Pat's warm hands tighter, listened to his murmuring and the growing noise in the corridors.

She felt her fear drip off her as warmth engulfed her.

The room grew bigger.

Pat got transparent, reshaped himself until Tabia felt like sitting in one of her beloved bubbles.

Floating through the air without effort.

She saw the bright rainbow colors swirling around an orb.

The warm breeze coming from outside the open window, had tides.

With the next ebb tide, her orb floated out of her former living room, past the light green, heart shaped leaves of the birches.

Tabia's orb floated higher. Green swirls dancing with blue and yellow ones.

She felt like dancing on a rainbow through the air.

Soon the mansion underneath was a mere memory.

Tabia looked forward to meeting Katherine, and discover the world outside her former one.

THE END

Excerpt:
The missing Jack O'Lantern

Humid and soft orange pumpkin meat clung at Vanessa's bare hands. Every inch of her hands, up to the elbows, nearly to her rolled up sleeves, was covered in the squishy meat, interwoven with pumpkin seeds. It seemed like the, promisingly of soup smelling, deep orange meat had a preference for her skin. The three to five year old children, sitting opposite the low, hardly higher than her knees, table, watched her prepare the fifth pumpkin. They had pulled out the easy stuff. Now she had to scrape the interior clean. They waited to create Jack O'Lanterns from them and learn how to use a knife, or so the teacher had explained it to Vanessa.

She silently hoped, none of the kindergarten children would cut open a finger or injure herself or a neighbor next to her. Yet, she had volunteered to come and help this afternoon preparing the pumpkins.

The children chattered about the faces they wanted to cut and stuff only they could understand.

Vanessa smiled and focused on scrubbing out more of the firm pumpkin meat, too hard for the children to get out and too thick for them to cut through with their small kitchen knifes.

Her concentration was not only on the pumpkins and the children though. She was well aware of the handsome man sitting next to her on an equally small chair. He had introduced himself as Marc, father of Angelique. Like herself, he scraped out an orange pumpkin. The difference? His arms were clean, as was most of the skin on his hands.

She wouldn't compare herself to another parent. Not in kindergarten! She had to stop that. She knew she couldn't compete with any of those humans around. They might be better with stuff like that, but she was surely better with technology. Or at least she had to. Otherwise, she would be stuck on this primitive planet forever. She wished for a brighter future for her daughter than to live with humans forever.

Excerpt end of: The missing Jack O'Lantern

More books

A tea shop taking cups, plates, and forks as payment. Not your everyday stop. More different than expected.

As a Tea Shop Owner with doors to various places, Amanda needs customers. Customers who pay with rare cups, plates, and forks.

Today, though, there is no customer. Thread lingers in her gut. She even got dressed, instead of greeting the first customer. Still with a speck of flour on her cheek in the early morning.

Amanda checks her magic doors in the world. She finds deserted places. Void of every sign of life.

A mysterious magic shop fantasy story.

His tongue feels sticky and dry in his mouth, glued to his gums by the dusty air.

Down-to-earth accountant Harald Amsun stands in the old, dust filled air. Generations of dust linger, ready to entomb him at his next movement.

Harald explores the ruinous house with the completely intact shutters. He longs to get it over and getting back to work. Quick.

Contrary to his usuall attitude the house tempts him. Raising long gone memories and mysteries.

An electrifying tale of an accountant whose choices change the house and his world. Irreversible.

Fantasy

Beaten Path in the Mist
Vampire Hunting with the Tiger Eye
Marlene's New Monster
Remorse of the Mermaid
Wipe off the Dust
The Book Burning
Stars Flying into Philosophy
Red: #890000

The True Mage Survives
The Flower on the Mountain Top
The speaking Mirror
The Fork with the Scales
Fairy Needs Courage
The Rainbow Bubble Collapse
Repair the Music
The missing Jack O'Lantern

Romance

World Cup and Pink Ropes
An Invitation to a Wedding
Corrupted Food Storage
Dance to your Love
Fighting the Cinnamon Guy
Forgotten Communications

The Magic Book
Love against all Rules
Love as a Christmas Present
The Griffin's Wedding Ring
Crossroads with Half the Information (Collection)

Science Fiction

Abandonned Time Travel
Alien Visit
Coloring an Apple
Corrupted Food Storage
Dicovery (Novel)
Red: #890000
Served like red Wine
Shards of her Life

Support Refused
Sweet Depths
The Water Theft
Lottery Win: The Third Set of Doors
Human Interactions Preferred
Intertwined Fate

www.ingramcontent.com/pod-product-compliance
Lightning Source LLC
Chambersburg PA
CBHW021404160726
47994CB00007B/3072